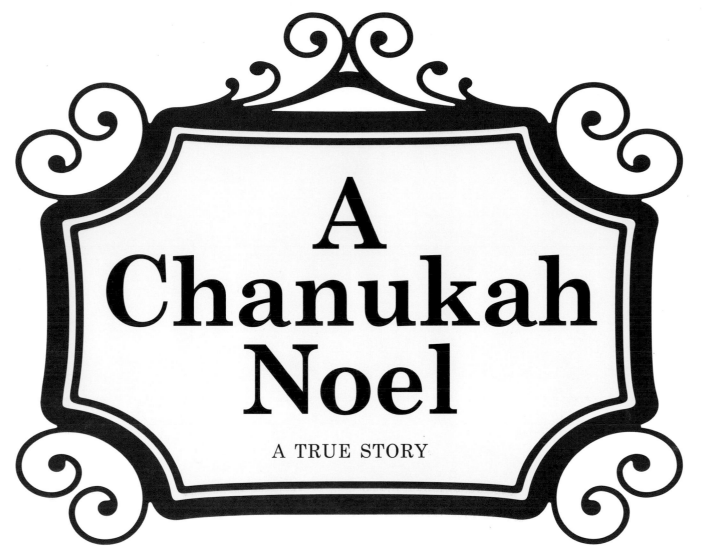

# A Chanukah Noel

### A TRUE STORY

WRITTEN BY SHARON JENNINGS

ILLUSTRATED BY GILLIAN NEWLAND

Second Story Press

One day, Daddy came home from work and said, "I have a big surprise. We are going to live in France." I wasn't so sure I liked this surprise, but I left home with Mommy and Daddy and sailed all the way across the ocean.

In our new life, many things were different.

For one thing, everyone spoke French except me, so I was placed in the lowest grade at school until I learned. I did not like this and said so.

And another thing – once we left the city of Paris to live in our little village, all our milk and cheese came straight from a farm instead of a grocery store. It smelled funny. I didn't like this either.

But every time I complained, Mommy said, "We are in France now, Charlotte. We will live like the French and be grateful for new opportunities."

The only thing I was grateful for was our snack at school – a large chunk of chocolate in a piece of chewy French bread called a *baguette*!

Most of my new schoolmates were kind but Colette was not. She called me *l'étrangère,* the foreigner, and laughed when I made mistakes in French.

"Don't worry," said Mommy. "You can study hard when the others have their holiday."

I frowned. I did not want to study hard when the others had their holiday. I wanted to have the holiday too. I complained again. "But Mommy, we are in France now. You said we should live like the French and be grateful for a new opportunity."

Mommy only laughed. "It is not a *French* holiday, honey. It is a *Christian* holiday. We are Jewish. We will celebrate Chanukah."

"Yes, but..."

Mommy raised her eyebrows, and I knew I had said enough.

But it was hard to keep quiet. It seemed that every house and shop was decorated with boughs of evergreens and holly and garlands of white lights.

All we had was our one small menorah for Chanukah.

The Christmas markets, called *marchés de Noël,* were crowded with people buying and sampling all sorts of meats and cheeses and cookies and cakes. Toys and decorations hung in the open-air stalls, and merchants offered samples of wonderful sweets and pastries. The delicious smells of cinnamon and chocolate filled the air, but envy filled my heart.

At school, at least, I was part of the Christmas fun.

I helped decorate our classroom. I sang the carols. I ate the special treats my new friends brought in to share.

It should have been enough. But it was not. I wanted to go into all the stores and come out with my arms filled with secrets and surprises to be tucked under the tree and given away.

On the last day of school, we each brought in a small gift. I presented my pot of raspberry jam to Mademoiselle LaBev.

"I will give the gifts a number," our teacher explained. "At the end of the day, each of you will pull a number out of this hat to see which gift you will take home."

Colette was still rummaging around in her bag. "Oh no!" she cried. "I...I forgot my gift. I am so sorry!"

I held my breath. We were one gift short. What if they asked me not to take part because I was Jewish?

But then Mademoiselle LaBev said, "Don't worry. I just happen to have one extra gift!" I smiled with relief.

I walked home with Jeanette and Marie, fingering the tiny toy rolling pin that was my gift. "How silly of Colette," I said. "How could she forget to bring a present?"

Marie shook her head. "She didn't forget it, Charlotte. She didn't have one to bring."

"She is very poor," explained Jeanette. "She will not have much of a Christmas, that one."

I felt very sulky. *Me either*, I thought.

That night we lit another candle on our menorah. I tried to feel grateful, but I couldn't get Christmas out of my head.

I thought of another approach.

"Couldn't we have Chanukah *and* Christmas?" I begged my parents.

Daddy looked very stern. "Charlotte, we do not celebrate Christmas. Is that understood?"

"Yes, Daddy," I mumbled.

I wondered if Colette's Papa said the same thing to her.

My thoughts were still dancing around in my head. At school we had heard about the Magi, those travelers from afar bearing gifts. We were from afar. We could bring gifts. We could...

"Daddy!" I cried. "Could we have a Christmas if we don't actually *have* it?" The words jumped out of my mouth. "I mean, if we gave it away to someone else?"

I told my parents about Colette. "Could we do all the Christmas things and give them to her?"

For the second time that day I held my breath. My parents looked at each other.

My father smiled. "It might just be possible. But we do not want to embarrass Colette's family. I will try to think of a way."

I jumped up and hugged him.

In the morning, Daddy and I went to speak to Mr. Levert. My father wished him a good day and then he asked him about his cow. And then he talked about the weather. I hopped from one foot to another until I couldn't wait any longer.

"Please, Monsieur Levert," I blurted out. "I have a favor to ask. We are Jewish and we do not celebrate Christmas. But I would give anything to have a tree and the decorations and all the special food." I took a deep breath. "And so, Monsieur, I was hoping that you would let my family do all the shopping and the cooking and then bring it to you. Please, Monsieur Levert?"

Monsieur Levert looked at my father.

And then it came to me in a flash. "It would really be a gift — from you to me," I said.

Colette's father smiled. Then my daddy smiled too, and they shook hands.

On Christmas Eve morning, we drove to town. The air was crisp and clean, and dark clouds held the promise of snow.

The markets were bustling. We bought cheese and breads and a big fat goose and a special Christmas cake called a *bûche de Noël* and all kinds of candies and sugared nuts and fruit. We selected a tree and decorations and a string of colored lights. And we chose a gift for everyone in the Levert family.

I bought Colette a doll with some of the coins I had received for Chanukah.

We hurried home to prepare. My mother had never cooked a goose before, and she had to make many phone calls for advice. My father chopped vegetables and peeled potatoes. I sat at the kitchen table, agonizing over how to wrap the gifts so each one would be special.

We arrived at the Leverts' in the late afternoon. Colette and her family came to the door, and I pointed to our sled filled to the brim.

"Happy Holiday! *Joyeux Noël!*" I shouted. "This is for you!"

We unloaded all our treasures and surprises and then my father said, "Come along, Charlotte. It is time for us to go."

I froze. I hadn't known that we were not going to be part of the celebrations. I stumbled down the steps quickly so Colette wouldn't see the tears in my eyes.

And then, the miracle!

"Wait!" Monsieur Levert called out. "We cannot accept your gift if you do not allow us to share it with you."

I stared at my father and finally – finally – he smiled.

Our fathers put up the tree, we hung the decorations, and gave out our presents.

And when Colette hugged her doll and said, "Merci, Charlotte" my heart was filled with joy, all the joy of Christmas and Chanukah together.

Library and Archives Canada Cataloguing in Publication

Jennings, Sharon
Chanukah Noel / by Sharon Jennings ; illustrated by Gillian
Newland.

ISBN 978-1-897187-74-6

I. Newland, Gillian  II. Title.

PS8569.E563C43 2010        jC813'.54        C2010-902512-1

*Second Story Press gratefully acknowledges the support of the
Ontario Arts Council and the Canada Council for the Arts for
our publishing program. We acknowledge the financial support
of the Government of Canada through the Book Publishing
Industry Development Program.*

Printed and bound in China

ONTARIO ARTS COUNCIL
CONSEIL DES ARTS DE L'ONTARIO

Canada Council    Conseil des Arts
for the Arts      du Canada

Published by
SECOND STORY PRESS
20 Maud Street, Suite 401
Toronto, Ontario, Canada
M5V 2M5
www.secondstorypress.ca

For Charlotte Teeple,
whose story this is.
—S.J.